~Nana's Birthday Party~

Amy Hest
Pictures by Amy Schwartz

Morrow Junior Books   New York

Watercolors and pencils were used for the full-color artwork.
The text type is 17-point Weiss.
Text copyright © 1993 by Amy Hest
Illustrations copyright © 1993 by Amy Schwartz

Printed in Singapore at Tien Wah Press.

1   2   3   4   5   6   7   8   9   10

Library of Congress Cataloging-in-Publication Data
Hest, Amy.
Nana's birthday party / Amy Hest; illustrated by Amy Schwartz.
p.   cm.
Summary: Maggie, who writes stories, and her cousin Brette, who
paints pictures, combine their talents to create the grandest
present ever for their grandmother Nana's birthday.
ISBN 0-688-07497-9 (trade).—ISBN 0-688-07498-7 (library)
[1. Grandmothers—Fiction.   2. Cousins—Fiction.   3. Authors—
Fiction.   4. Artists—Fiction.   5. Birthdays—Fiction.]
I. Schwartz, Amy, ill.   II. Title.
PZ7.H4375Nan   1993
[E]—dc20   92-10260   CIP   AC

To the family Schaye
—A. H.

For Monica and Lydia
—A. S.

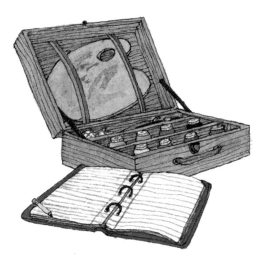

Every year, halfway between Christmas and Thanksgiving, Nana makes herself a birthday party. It's a grand occasion, that party, with relatives from every borough and Nana's birthday rules tacked to the door—rules such as NO JEANS. NO GUM. NO PRESENTS, EXCEPT THE KIND YOU MAKE YOURSELF. NO FIGHTING AND NO WHINING.

Nana lives smack in the middle of New York City. Her apartment is so big you can run from room to room for different city views. The dark wood floors are so shiny you can skim and glide like a skater when you're wearing just socks.

And those ceilings! Nana's are so high you can jump away on any bed and never ever hit your head. That is, you can jump away until she hollers *Stop!* in the doorway.

The night before Nana's party, I get to sleep over. So does my cousin Brette. Brette's mother and mine are sisters, and *their* mother is Nana.

The fastest way to Nana's is the subway, and there are fourteen stops from our station to hers. At 86th Street, Mama and I climb all those millions of stairs to the street. It is dark already and the lamps in Central Park make hazy shadows in the cold wet fog.

"This year, I'm giving Nana something really special. A story, Mama, and I am writing it myself. But first," I say in my worried voice, "I have to think up an idea."

Mama slips woolen mittens over my fingers, then slips on her own. "Well, you do write splendid stories, Maggie."

"I know. But Brette's presents are always better."

"Different, not better." Mama takes my hand and my pink valise and we walk to Nana's, hunched against the cold.

"Good evening," call the doormen, Jack and Jed. They look just alike.

"Good evening to you!" My mother bows a funny bow.

Jack and Jed have minded this door for a hundred years, I think. They know my mother because this is the building where she was a girl. They always kid around and say things like, "You're still a girl as far as we're concerned." And they always laugh at their own jokes.

I spin into the old-time elevator. There's a little seat in the corner. Just in case you're tired.

Nana's front door is dotted with holly.

"It's about time!" She folds her arms around us. "Brette's been here an hour."

"You are looking grand," says my mother to her mother.

"Don't I always?" Nana hangs my coat in the coat closet that looks like a flower garden.

"Are you killing yourself with too much work?" says my mother to her mother.

"Boss!" Nana laughs, waving a hand in the air.

"Me boss *you*?" My mother laughs, too. "Not a chance!"

Those two love to talk about who's the boss of whom.

Nana walks so fast. On the way to the kitchen, she pulls lipstick from her apron pocket. Dab. Dab. Nana always wears red lipstick, no matter what, and she always has a list:

BAKE CAKE...HANG STREAMERS...ICE THE CAKE...
SET TABLES...BLOW UP BALLOONS....

"Halloooo!" My cousin Brette is stretched, all of her, across the kitchen counter. I can't believe she fits. There is chocolate

on her nose and flour streaked into that long red hair.

"How's the cake?" I say.

"Excellent." Brette smacks her lips.

My mother dips two fingers in the bowl of batter.
"Divine!" she agrees and dips again.

Then Nana calls her "worse than a kid" and shoos her out
the door until tomorrow.

An overnight at Nana's means sleeping in the room that once was our mothers'. Every single thing in it used to be our mothers'—the beds and dressers and rolltop desk, the rows of books and tiers of bears in lacy bear dresses. Right next door is a bathroom with diamond tiles on the floor and an ancient tub on stubby feet.

I unbuckle my valise.

Brette wants to see my notebook, I can tell. This notebook has a red leather cover and it goes everywhere I go. Brette yawns but I know it's a pretend yawn. I know she wants to touch my book and read everything inside.

"I guess you made something swell for Nana. You always do," I say.

"Not this year." Brette flops back. Her feet go up and she pedals the air. "I couldn't think of a single thing."

"Not *one* thing?"

Brette arches her back like an upside-down cat. "*You* make all the good presents," she says. "Like that macaroni necklace two birthdays ago, and the pebble collage the year before that."

"But you're the one who paints." I make a long sighing sound through my lips. "Nana keeps all your pictures and she puts them over the fireplace in real frames, not construction-paper frames."

Brette smiles. I know what she's thinking. She's thinking about painting a picture for Nana. And I'm thinking it's going to be gorgeous, and that makes me mad. Brette's pictures are too good. She's got a real paint set, the kind that grown-ups use. It comes with two paintbrushes and special little jars of color. Brette takes that paint set everywhere, and her easel, too. It folds right up and she carries it on the subway, even.

I find Nana on top of a high ladder.

"Better not fall," I say.

"Better not tell your mother." Nana strings colorful streamers from one end of the living room to the other. She goes up and down and up, stringing streamers until it looks like a birthday.

"Brette paints better than anyone I know," I call up the ladder. "Better even than some grown-ups."

"And you write stories, Maggie." Nana reaches for tape. "Each to her own."

"But if I could paint the way she does…"

"…Then you wouldn't be my Maggie." Nana climbs down. "I would miss the way you weave words into sentences that are lovely to read."

She sits on the bottom step of the ladder. Elbows on knees. Chin in hands. Nana is thinking about the next thing on her list, I bet. Not me. I am thinking about how to fill my notebook with a story.

"Streamers!" Brette skates in, singing away in blue-star socks. "I love streamers!"

"Balloons next." Nana takes a bag of them from the cupboard. That's where she keeps the hatbox with old pictures. I swear, that hatbox is more fun than candy!

So, instead of blowing air in balloons, we all squeeze

close on the big old couch near the window. There
must be a thousand photos here, including plenty of
our mothers.

"Remember," Nana says, "every picture tells a story."

Brette holds up a yellowed one with curling edges.
"What's the story here?" she asks.

Nana takes a close look. "Well, here I am, dancing away like Ginger Rogers in a gown…and look at this…cousin Judy's wedding. Here's your mother, Brette, this girl with whipped cream on her nose. She was very big on the color green that year. The dress she chose was *very* fancy." Nana shakes her head. "Over here is Maggie's mother. You can see that she is frowning and pouting. Why? Because *she* wanted to wear pants that looked like the kind of overalls you'd wear on a farm! I said you can't wear those to a wedding and she was mad…."

I love hearing stories about my mother when she was a girl. It's hard to believe she was once my size.

After balloons, Brette and I head for the room that used to be our mothers', turning on lamps as we go. We wriggle into the space between our beds. Brette's easel is all set up. Her pots of paint are waiting for a painter.

Whenever Brette paints, she twirls her hair around two fingers. She wears a real artist's smock with lots of smudges. She frowns and sometimes she smiles. And she talks away.

"I am painting a picture of two girls and their mother," she begins. "They are on their way to a wedding…"

"…But before they go on the subway"—I drum my
pencil on the carpet—"they stop off at the *carousel* in their
fancy clothes. Each girl gets a ride on a painted horse, and so
does their mother.

"Imagine them, all dressed up for a wedding, but riding on a painted horse!"

I write away in my notebook while Brette paints at her easel. She uses up a lot of green.

Much later we staple my writing and Brette's pictures together like a book. We make a red-and-green cover and tape Nana's old-time photograph to the front and call it *Two Girls and Their Mother and Cousin Judy's Wedding*.

After that, we sneak around the apartment, every single
room and hallway of it, to track down tape and tissue paper.
We take turns wrapping Nana's grandest birthday present
ever. We hide it for tomorrow.

Then Brette and I fill the tub with bubbles and hop right in until Nana calls us to supper.